KT-385-217

To my grandsons, Nat and Will. Also, love and thanks to my brother, John, for valuable advice   HC

To my mother, D. K. Holabird, and the Bateau St Georges   KH

PUFFIN BOOKS

Published by the Penguin Group
Penguin Books Ltd, 80 Strand, London WC2R 0RL, England
Penguin Group (USA), Inc., 375 Hudson Street, New York, New York 10014, USA
Penguin Books Australia Ltd, 250 Camberwell Road, Camberwell, Victoria 3124, Australia
Penguin Books Canada Ltd, 10 Alcorn Avenue, Toronto, Ontario, Canada M4V 3B2
Penguin Books India (P) Ltd, 11 Community Centre, Panchsheel Park, New Delhi – 110 017, India
Penguin Group (NZ), cnr Airborne and Rosedale Roads, Albany, Auckland 1310, New Zealand
Penguin Books (South Africa) (Pty) Ltd, 24 Sturdee Avenue, Rosebank 2196, South Africa

Penguin Books Ltd, Registered Offices: 80 Strand, London WC2R 0RL, England

www.penguin.com

First published 2004
9 10 8

Copyright © HIT Entertainment plc, 2004
Text copyright © Katharine Holabird, 2004
Illustrations copyright © Helen Craig Ltd, 2004
Angelina, Angelina Ballerina and the Dancing Angelina logo are trademarks of HIT Entertainment plc, Katharine Holabird and Helen Craig Ltd.
Angelina is registered in the UK, Japan and US Pat. & TM. Off. The dancing Angelina logo is registered in the UK.
All rights reserved.

The moral right of the author and illustrator has been asserted

Manufactured in China by South China Printing Ltd. Co.

Without limiting the rights under copyright reserved above, no part of this publication may be reproduced, stored in or introduced into a retrieval system, or transmitted, in any form or by any means (electronic, mechanical, photocopying, recording or otherwise), without the prior written permission of both the copyright owner and the above publisher of this book

British Library Cataloguing in Publication Data
A CIP catalogue record for this book is available from the British Library

ISBN 0–141–38015–2

To find out more about Angelina, visit her web site at **www.angelinaballerina.com**

Angelina, Star of the Show

Story by **Katharine Holabird** Illustrations by **Helen Craig**

PUFFIN

"Welcome on board *The Jolly Rat*, Angelina," said Grandma and Grandpa. "Are you ready to set off for the Mouseland Dance Festival?"

"I can't wait," said Angelina. "I'm going to think up a special dance on the way, so I can be the star of the show! Do you like my costume?"

"It's lovely, but we need all paws on deck to get the boat to the festival," Grandpa reminded her as he started the engine.

But Angelina wasn't listening. She skipped around
the deck, imagining her great performance.

"Aren't you going to wear your overalls?" asked Grandma,
in surprise. Angelina smiled sweetly and shook her head.

"I've decided to stay in my costume," she said.

As *The Jolly Rat* chugged along through the countryside, Angelina twirled and danced, stopping only to pester her grandparents with questions:

"What do you think of this step?" Angelina asked, and "Does this look nice?"

"You're a sailor now," Grandma reminded her sternly, but Angelina was too busy dancing to be a sailor.

"*The Jolly Rat* needs a new coat of paint,"
Grandpa announced, and he handed
Angelina a paintbrush.

"But Grandpa, I really *have* to practise. I've got a whole new
dance routine to think up!" said Angelina, and she spun
into Grandpa's tin of paint and waltzed off, leaving
little footprints all over the deck!

After that, Grandpa decided Angelina should help Grandma
down in the galley, but Angelina forgot to watch the soup
while she practised pliés and it all boiled over.

That afternoon, Angelina worked on her arabesques and it wasn't long before she got all tangled up in Grandma's washing and Grandpa's fishing line. She had to be rescued by both her grandparents, who were getting very grumpy. "That's enough, Angelina!" they cried.

When Angelina went
to bed that night, she promised
Grandma and Grandpa that she would
stop dancing, but the very next morning she forgot,
and performed a magnificent series of leaps along the deck.

The deck was slippery and Angelina lost her balance.
She tumbled right into a can of oil and
got covered from head to toe in
horrible black grease.

"Oh no – look what I've done!"
Angelina gasped. Her beautiful costume was ruined.

Angelina was so horrified that she raced below deck to her bunk bed and cried her heart out. Then, just when she had decided she was the worst mouseling in the world, Grandma came to give her a cuddle.

"I'm sorry, Grandma!" Angelina sobbed.
"I haven't been very helpful, have I?"

"I know you're sorry," said Grandma, as she dried Angelina's tears.

"I haven't got anything to wear to the dance festival now," sniffed Angelina. "And I can't do my dance without a costume!"

"Well, let's see what's in my old chest," suggested Grandma.
And there, inside the chest, they found a beautiful sailor suit.

"That was my favourite outfit," Grandma said,
"and that's me wearing it," she added proudly,
pointing to a faded photograph that was
hanging on the wall.

"Ooh," gasped Angelina excitedly.
"Do you think I could borrow
it if I'm very careful?"

"Of course," smiled Grandma,
"I'll add some special ribbons."

For the rest of the journey, Angelina wore her old overalls, and she tried very hard to be a real sailor.

Before long, she could steer *The Jolly Rat* down the Mousetail Canal.

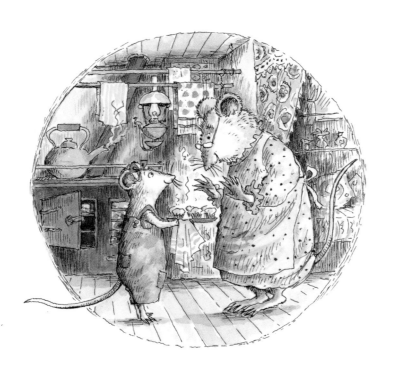

She swabbed the decks and painted the woodwork with Grandpa, and she cooked with Grandma down in the galley.

She even baked her grandparents some Cheddar cheese pies!

And in the evenings after supper, while Grandpa played his penny whistle, Grandma showed Angelina some of her favourite dances.

"Thank you, Grandma," said Angelina one night, "you've given me a wonderful idea."

A few days later, *The Jolly Rat* arrived at the Mouseland Dance Festival
with a new coat of paint and all decked out in garlands of flowers.

Angelina proudly tooted the horn.
"We're here!" she shouted.

As the festival opened, Grandpa played his penny whistle and Angelina performed her new dance. It was a special sailor's jig that she'd practised with Grandma. The crowds loved the show and cheered for more.

"Hooray for the little sailor!" they shouted.

When the evening was over, Angelina hugged her grandparents.

"You really were the star of the show," said Grandma.

"And you're the very best Grandma and Grandpa in the whole of Mouseland!" Angelina replied.

Then they all joined paws and skipped happily back to *The Jolly Rat*.